As a Friend

Other Books by Forrest Gander

POETRY
Eye Against Eye
The Blue Rock Collection
Torn Awake
Science & Steepleflower
Deeds of Utmost Kindness
Lynchburg
Rush To The Lake

ESSAYS
A Faithful Existence: Reading, Memory, & Transcendence

COLLABORATIVE BOOKS WITH ARTISTS
A Clearing (with Ray Meeks)
Las Canchas (with Dan Borris)
TopSoil (with Ray Meeks)
Sound of Summer Running (with Ray Meeks)
12 X Twelve (with Tjibbe Hooghiemstra)

TRANSLATION
Firefly Under the Tongue, Selected Poems of Coral Bracho
The Night, A Poem by Jaime Saenz (with Kent Johnson)
Another Kind of Tenderness, Xue Di
    (with Keith Waldrop, et. al.)
No Shelter: The Selected Poems of Pura López Colomé
Immanent Visitor: Selected Poems of Jaime Saenz
    (with Kent Johnson)

AS EDITOR
Ten Significant American Poets (Bosnia-Herzegovina)
Connecting Lines: New Poetry from Mexico (translation editor)
The Battlefield Where the Moon Says I Love You
    (second edition editor)
Mouth To Mouth: Poems by 12 Contemporary
    Mexican Women

As a Friend

BY FORREST GANDER

A NEW DIRECTIONS BOOK

The Publisher wishes to thank Lauren Abrams
for her assistance with this edition.

Book Design by Sylvia Frezzolini Severance
Manufactured in the United States of America
First published as a New Directions Paperbook Original
(NDP1104) in 2008.
Published simultaneously in Canada by Penguin Books Canada Limited
New Directions Books are printed on acid-free paper.

Library of Congress Cataloging-in-Publication Data

Gander, Forrest, 1956–
  As a friend / Forrest Gander.
    p. cm.
  ISBN 978-0-8112-1745-3 (pbk. : acid-free paper)
  1. Friendship—Fiction. I. Title.
  PS3557.A47A9 2008
  813'.54—dc22
                                    2008023125

New Directions Books are published for James Laughlin
by New Directions Publishing Corporation,
80 Eighth Avenue, New York 10011

"But perhaps all books are simply the written expression of a friendship searching for itself in the friendship of a stranger become our double: adversary and accomplice."

—Edmond Jabès, *The Book of Margins*
translated by Rosmarie Waldrop

For Brian Evenson

TABLEAUX

As a Friend

The Birth

And where is he, the biological father of the unborn child? States away. On a New Orleans tugboat in violent Gulf water. Nor will he make it so far up the river again, with five weeks' pay and anaconda boots, looking for a lovely girl's ear to nibble, and with half a notion, steadily declining, to betroth his charismatic loathsomeness to whatever sad someone might part her lips for him, take in his torrent of lies, and mistake him for whatever he surely is not.

The mother of the pregnant girl (some would say child) places her *King James* on the cane chair outside the second-floor door. Then she enters the room.

In the same glance by which she recognizes her daughter, in a cotton gown and long socks, flailing on the gurney, moaning Oh God Oh God, she sees the empty metal stirrups poking like weird levers from the gurney's sides. She hears her daughter's moans and fixes her eyes on the stirrups which seem, in their cold metallic gleaming, in her fatigue and anxiety, to authorize her daughter's suffering.

Oh honey. Dry-mouthed, the widow stands just inside the door and her sympathetic address, lacking sufficient force of utterance, dissipates in the air. Her daughter, not noticing her entrance, rocks on her hands and knees now between the gleaming stirrups, she pants, facing the wall, wiping her face against the mattress. Gasping, she rolls to her side, worn out and huge, her protuberant navel poking like a rivet head through the thin gown. At the front of the gurney, an aide, no older than the girl in labor, wipes a strand of brown hair from her own cheek, her shoulders slumped.

Meanwhile, the pregnant girl groans and rolls onto her back and her fingers clench the mattress. There is a stool along the far wall, a second long-limbed teenage aide atop it, her legs uncurling and curling around the stool's posts as she surveys the spectacle. Her nonchalance suggests that she has seen it all before. She casts a quick glance toward the widow frozen at the door. Their eyes meet. Then the aide stops chewing her gum and turns again to the incredible belly.

From the sink and basin in the room's far corner strides the midwife, horse-black hair, a young woman though twice the age of her two aides. She is wringing out a white washcloth. Sitting on the gurney's edge, she wipes spittle from the mouth of the girl in labor. Not acknowledging the presence of the widow with so much as a nod. After a minute, setting the washcloth aside, the midwife strokes the girl's hand and speaks to her in an undertone.

She has no right to judge me, the widow hears herself thinking.

Below the washbasin, some old quilts lie folded on the floor. Still moored to the door, rocking unsteadily on her heels, the widow recognizes the Drunk-Love-in-a-Cabin pattern on top. During the summer and fall of her husband's fatal sickness, she had taken up quilting on the porch, and slept there as well, wrapped in an unfinished pattern night after night, unable to endure the stench of infirmity within.

Now she has entered a room where her daughter's belly eclipses every image of herself, and she is not sure how to proceed. She feels superfluous, incapable of reconciling herself to this setback. She raised the girl to know better. But her daughter seemed bent on incarnating every potential disappointment that could be imagined, arguing with her teachers, refusing to go to church, sneaking the car out at night with no license. Where had she learned to drive? In the last few months, eating, sulking, expanding, the girl had spoken less and less as though her energies, the remnants of her youth, were being sucked inward and consumed. As if the infant were drawing off whatever was left of a cordial relationship between the widow and her daughter. And sometimes, it seemed to the widow that her daughter had pent up her feelings

as a punishment, as though she, her mother, were
somehow to blame.

Her teeth are chattering and the widow glances
again at the quilts on the floor. Somebody should
get one. Then she sees—how could she have looked
away—the tremendous belly transforming. She sees
it mound dramatically, drawing the girl's head and
shoulders forward toward her rising hips. The legs
spread and the gown rises to expose a strange mac-
ula of iodined flesh, anus and vagina, two dark
heartshapes. Visible from the larger, a thin trickle
of blood.

The aide on her stool stops chewing gum.

The other girl pauses at the sink with a wet
compress. Slowly, the midwife lays her hand on
the enormous belly. And just as her palm alights, a
jet of water bursts from between the thighs with a
pop.

In the next minutes, the widow feels her disin-
volvement grow exaggerated. She watches the second aide leap from her stool, snatching up from the
counter an armful of towels. Spreading them across
the soaked mattress. The midwife takes the wet,
swollen ankles and crosses them, crosses the daughter's legs, repeating calmly, Breathe, don't push;
breathe, don't push.

And now the daughter's screaming begins, the high shrill stabs of a dog whistle, barely audible. Then contractions punch her breath away. Soon she pales and furiously curses not her momma, not the derelict father, but the girls who have taken positions on both sides of the gurney to turn her onto her side. The daughter howls a string of outrageous execrations involving the Lord's name the likes of which the widow never has heard.

Oh, my god! Goddamn! It's shitsure ripping me apart. Then in whispers, My insides are! Coming out! Oh god oh god.

She grunts and seizes.

Don't do that, whines one of the girls scoldingly. You'll hurt the baby's head!

But she grunts and tightens again and pushes and the midwife declares, It's alright.

They lift her legs into the stirrups and bind them with buckled belts twice on the foot and twice at the thigh.

Push into your bottom, the midwife instructs. That's right, honey, go ahead and push. The midwife's hand on her naked knee. Her steady voice instructing the girls to massage the daughter's feet and calves.

But the contractions keep no rhythm, they are like a volcano inside her. An hour passes, seizures gripping the girl, overawing her. Her mother, fifteen feet away, remains motionless as the effigy of a spectator, transfixed by the quarter-sized opening between her daughter's iodized thighs where a patch of cheesy hair now begins to press outward. The vagina round as a steel ring, its thin inner membrane shining.

The daughter pushes, exhausted, her body like an animal on top of her, devouring her. Not coming, she begs. Not coming out! Can't breathe!

Her eyes widen and she doesn't take a breath. Can't breathe, she gasps. Going. To dying. And she strains for tiny sucks of air against some invisible clamp on her chest.

The widow wants to get closer, but she needs the solid door behind her against which she stands pressed.

She's dilated, the midwife says. And she pauses, the tips of her fingers within the swollen vagina, cupping a lanuginous patch of head.

The room smells deep to the widow, but not of anything she can say. Of something wrong, perhaps. It is like her own body odor intensified.

Push, the midwife is urging.

The daughter gulps for air, gasps, My back. God Jesus!

And this time the widow unplies herself from the door and marches straight toward the bed and slides her hand under the soaking gown, under the small of back and she rubs upwards into the hot coals of her daughter's arched spine. Her daughter whines, a short, breathless, abstract noise. And the woman banks her fingers against the long scarp, the swell of muscle on either side of the vertebrae, and draws her fingertips upward to the middle of the bowed back. Her child makes a sound as deaf people make, rolling against the widow's fingers. She flinches, the older woman, but maneuvers her hand upward again. She traces the wing-like shoulder blade with her thumb and it separates slightly and she can feel its beveled underside. Then she closes her eyes, transferring strength through her hands in an act of prayer, a prayer by which she would divert the moment's welter. Again, her fingertips smooth the long troughs between her daughter's ribs, the wet delta above the kidneys, the widow's knuckles wedged between the hot sheet and the flesh that heats it.

Aglow with sweat, the daughter holds her breath and her eyes break away from all of them toward the ceiling, beyond the ceiling. They focus wildly on a pain that is no one else's.

Looking from her beet-red face downward, the widow can see for herself the bones of her daughter's pelvis giving way. Spreading like syrup.

Breathe! Breathe! You're doing this to yourself! the midwife snaps. One of the aides, swallowing her gum, echoes her crazily.

Breathe! Breathe! she implores, looking about frantically, as though someone might halt the imminent tragedy in order to reassure her.

And the daughter draws in a cluster of tiny sips of air, quick shudders like a car over gravel, mouthing the words, Save me, Save me, her body contorted into a relentless spasm.

All the mother has never thought begins to pour out of her. I love you, I forgive you, I love you, forgive me. And the girl simultaneously mouthing, I'm dying, I'm dying, her face a hideous garnet.

You can breathe! Breathe! the midwife barks. The girl's eyes roll back, her terror fixed on nothing in the room.

At which point an electrical failure spirals

along the nape of the older woman's neck and her brain flickers behind her eyes. She stumbles backwards, backwards, feeling backwards with her blind hands behind her. Backs into the wall like a sightless animal, her face drained utterly. Down she slides not wanting to lose consciousness, down the wall, knees buckling, haunches patting the floorboards, chin nutating into bosom, yet straining in her mind to stay present.

Which is when the head begins to sweep out, the perineum dilating around it to thin transparency. A shriek.

Burns! It burns!

As though a thread were pulled away, thin bright blood flicks toward her left flank as the perineum rips. Body contracting in short pushes, the breath returning, she begins to pant through her teeth like a mad beast, past all screaming.

Baby forehead, top of brow, face covered in white grease. A pause in its descent. The midwife supporting the weird head at the vagina, saying Stop, stop pushing, stop now, don't push.

Probing with her fingers and finding the umbilical cord, a length around the throat. The baby's face screwed sideways, dark purple under a chalky mask, the section of cord visible to the mid-wife, bluish and vesselled.

She speaks to her assistants. Reaches into her smock and hands something white to each of them.

Why, these are shoelaces, one says.

From the widow collapsed against the wall, a gurgle. Inhuman noises.

The midwife wedges the syringe into the infant's mouth while the girls tie off the cord. She repositions the syringe, releasing the bulb. Withdraws it, squeezes it onto the floor. Pokes it into a tiny nostril. The other. Then she brings the scissors from her smock and cuts the cord, one quick bloody spurtle. Twists the head a quarter turn and unwraps the sausage-like length of cord.

Now push hard! Now do it! the midwife orders. Supporting the head with one hand and pressing down on it with the other, she flinches as she feels the instant of the baby's collarbone breaking. Push, push! One at a time, shoulders emerging. Push! The body whooshes out. Prune face, wrinkled flesh in bloody vernix.

It's a boy, she thinks and wonders if she has spoken aloud. Purple rubber doll, dead-looking.

He kicks and she drops him and catches him before he falls.

A peculiar faraway catwail beginning. And everything suddenly at a distance. The midwife drifting into a wholesale unmindfulness. God help me, she thinks vaguely. Above the tiny piercing yowl that seems to come not from the little jerking weight between her two palms but from every corner of the room, she hears the daughter weeping. The one aide choking and coughing. The other absolutely silent.

Against the wall, the older woman has lost them in a rich spiritual failure, and she cannot stand.

* * *

The young mother's memory of the birth is incoherent. The event singes her so profoundly that it leaves little residue, a bleat of time in which her acting self displaced the self that watches, judges, records. Although she preserves a repertoire of images, and one unforgettable sound, she has no way to process them, to integrate them into the main chapters of her life. Her life moves on. The intense fragments of those hours she thought would kill her are gradually replaced by a furtive curiosity.

As for the infant, he disappears. Someone adopts him. The birth mother tells herself, as she turns nineteen, twenty-one, twenty-four, twenty-eight, that she does not long for him. But each waking day, she imagines him, and sometimes in strange dreams. Even after she marries and has other children. She imagines him. Her lost boy. Whatever became of him?

Clay:
Landscape with a Man Being Killed by a Snake

es let himself in without knocking and two at a time shot up the stairs like he was escaping a bear. I heard the clang of his ring on the banister, the pitch of his footfall rising. He entered the living room through the kitchen and ceremoniously placed a piece of paper on the door-on-four-cinderblocks that served for a table by the couch where I was rolling a joint. It's for you, he said.

Les liked staging dramatic interactions from which he could exit quickly, leaving a charged space behind him. His resonance. He would punctuate the remarkable things he said with silences, his extravagant gestures with absence. Looking back, I imagine that he was practicing his death. And when he came into my apartment that night and handed me a poem, he was securing my role in it.

I thought then: he loves me. That's what this means. That's why he drove here to give me this piece of paper with a poem on it and then say he had to go. I thought: we have an incomparable intimacy. He wrote something for me.

The poem was titled "The Plot."

17

* * *

At that time, Les was the only one of us who was married, and he'd already been married twice, a flat out mystery to me. It had to have been the fact of his adoption, his uncertainty about family, some hunger to be loved. Maybe an undertow of anxiety that no one could see led him to formalize an idea about how adults were supposed to act: if you lived with a woman, you married her and then you had kids. It was curiously old-fashioned.

But other women didn't leave Les alone, nor he them. Come-ons, experiments, tendril passions. I remember him telling me that one life didn't allow for the possibilities of one man. As if I had settled for something less than he had.

His second wife's name was Cora. No one among our friends had known the first, his high-school sweetheart.

Few of us knew Cora either. She lived on the small farm her parents bequeathed her, across the state line in Pineville, Missouri. She's a painter, Les would say. But otherwise, he didn't talk about her. Their phone number was either unlisted or more probably, considering Les's penchant for mysteries, listed under an alias. At least three times a month, Les would drive into Missouri to see Cora "at the farm." So he let on to me once when we were surveying. He'd somehow convinced Cora that the farm was a better place for her to paint, that Eureka Springs was where he needed to live for work, and that Sarah, who everyone in Eureka Springs knew was not only his roommate, but his lover, was a militant lesbian who paid her share of the rent but was rarely around. In any case, on those evenings when the survey crew fell together at Lana's Café for dinner, Les would always make a call to his wife from the pay phone near the bathrooms. Presumably, it would have been awkward to call her from the house he shared with Sarah.

And even though Les was married to Cora and living with Sarah, it was fairly clear to everyone else that he was making the rounds. With the potter, the folk singer, the bartender.

I caught him in the Lyric theater, sitting in back, making out with someone I didn't recognize. In the dark, I wouldn't have distinguished Les except that he hurried in with her just before the lights fully dimmed and I knew his shape and the way he moved, rolling on the balls of his feet, all swing and curve like a big cat. Before the previews were finished, they were in the same seat.

That was something I wouldn't have thought to do. To fuck in the back of a movie theater.

I sat there, hardly watching the movie, thinking that while his mouth was wet with her wetness, whoever she was, and hers with his, I was alone as usual, slumped in the dark, my fingers and lips smeared with the grease they poured on my popcorn and called butter.

* * *

I never heard him read anything he'd written, but he would sometimes quote a poem, his own or someone else's, in conversation. It sounds unlikely, self-conscious or pretentious or bogus, but across the booth from us at The High Hat, he could join the lines of a poem to the flow of talk seamlessly. His face was so weighted down by its brooding handsomeness that he seemed older and more convincing than the rest of us. His *gravitas* sucked us in. He could lock his eyes on you and draw you toward an alien realm where you were given to suspend your habits of thought. It was as if he'd come from a place where excitement wasn't taken to be a reverse indicator of intelligence and where it was normal to mention Cocteau and blue channel catfish in the same sentence. None of us had his range, none of us had read so much. The opal blackness of his eyes was magnetic.

Everyone knows how much I love you. All your gestures have become my gestures. I remember him quoting those lines one night at The High Hat. What I mostly remember of those days are particular things he said. His words didn't memorialize events so much as events enabled him to practice a way of talking that mesmerized us, even when we knew it was bullshit.

I have no doubt that at least half of what he said was exactly that. The things he'd mention as if in passing: how he'd earned money teaching police officers karate, how he met Ingmar Bergman's cinematographer on his one trip to New York, how that same weekend, he spent the night with Alvin Ailey's principle dancer who, he said, kicked him out of bed in the morning, staring at him as if he were crazy when he asked if he could see her again. These were the kind of inventions a quality liar who rarely crossed the state line might tell gullible friends with equally limited experience. I'm sure he practiced in the mirror the set of his jaw and his hieratic gaze.

Nevertheless, I'd find myself trying to mimic his down-turned lips and his slow, smoky voice, retelling his stories, where I thought I could get away with it, as if they were my own.

Everyone knew how much I loved him.

* * *

It was a typical June day. I downshifted into second at the square by The Basin Hotel where the old men had set up their lawn chairs in a little circle and joined yesterday's conversation to this morning's whittling, fragrant cedar shavings already flecking their loafers. Someone with a straw hat stood with his back to his chair, plucked his trousers above the knees, and sat down. I parked next to three mud-caked pickups in the gravel lot behind the pottery studio and backtracked the half block to Walker Land Surveyor. A ten-speed leaned against the wall outside the door and two orange dragonflies idled on the wet concrete windowsill beneath the air conditioner. Quinton Walker was in the side room talking to a rancher about a boundary job. I could hear him saying, *Yeah, we'll definitely get down there next week*, as I came in past the draft table and the ratty chairs into the kitchen and poured a cup of coffee. *Sure we're definitely going to get down there next week*, I parroted, announcing myself. He stuck his pony-tailed head into the doorway and gave me a look.

I tore open two sugars, courtesy of Frank's Truck Stop, and poured them in. After stirring with my little finger, I watched a dirty swirl eddy across the black surface. I carried the Styrofoam cup into the back room where there was another

23

long draft table covered with plats and, protected from dust by a Union Jack, an old plotter machine. On the radio, a reporter was describing survivors on a boat that had set out from a refugee camp only to be attacked by pirates.

From the shelf along the back wall, I grabbed one of the yellow two-ways and put it in my side pocket next to my calculator. I took an extra battery for the EDM and carried it, with my coffee and Quinton's keys, which were on the counter in the kitchen, back outside, and I walked toward Quinton's Chevy C-10, my warped reflection in his hubcap. I got in on the passenger side, leaving the door ajar. A fat yellow cat jumped onto the hood and then up onto the roof.

The rancher went by, mimed tipping his hat, and got into his truck. The cat reversed its earlier trajectory, drumming the hood as it descended, and then dawdled up the wooden stairs toward the pottery studio. A few minutes later, Quinton lowered the tailgate and shoved the bright orange theodolite and meter cases onto the truck bed. Then he opened the driver's door. Wait a minute, he said, I should bring a print.

We headed to a small job in Green Forest where there were about a dozen tiny WPA-era natural stone cabins just off the highway. The reflection of trees cascaded up the windshield relentless-ly. Fifty feet before the cabins, we passed two signs advertising an antique shop. The smaller sign was an oversized cut-out of an Ozark rocking chair. But the post under the chair sign had tilted—maybe a car backed into it, I thought—so that the image of the chair blocked out the last word on the bigger sign. Instead of reading *Stop Here for Good Bargains*, it now read *Stop Here for Good*.

Quinton sniggered. With pebbles dinging the under-chassis, he pulled into the horseshoe drive-way that serviced the cluster of cabins soon to be dozed.

Yeah, I saw it, I said, unimpressed. You and Les messed with their signs?

Quinton glanced out the side window to keep from snorting directly at me.

Why didn't you set the breaklines then?

Theodolite got hot, I was hungover as hell. The whole day was basically fucked by ten, Quinton answered. Ended up we drove by the golf course, Les made me park while he took a shit in the six hole.

Quinton stomped the emergency brake and as

we let ourselves out of the truck, I caught the rank whiff of my underarms.

The morning was gorgeous. Between the cabin and the road, an apple tree was in bloom. I looked around the parking lot and spotted the flagged control point that Quinton or Les had hammered into the busted macadam.

Jesus Christ, Quinton.

Quinton came over and stood beside me staring at the black ants swarming around a hole about three inches from the control point. He said, Clay, you know I wouldn't have put that point there if the ants had been there. You bring bug spray?

No.

Maybe you could stand on something, he said. Must be going to rain, they're getting their business done early.

* * *

I would guess that Les was a liar not just because it was expedient, but because he took lying to be creative. He lied not only about his wife Cora, his girlfriend Sarah, his lovers, but about everything. I heard him lie to the man we were supposed to meet at ten a.m. about a surveying job, when at ten a.m. he was screwing around with the bartender and didn't pick me up until after eleven. He lied so fluently, with such an instinct for the unexpected detail, he could make me think he'd seen a movie I knew for a fact he didn't see. He lied to the editor who had paid him to conduct an interview he'd never done with some famous writer. He'd lie about a jar of peanut butter in Quinton's office kitchen. He had a perfect ear. He could imitate any bird, and he was the first bird watcher I ever knew. He could walk out of Bergman's *Wild Strawberries*—after convincing us to drive to Fayetteville to watch it, talking up the movie into an event we would sooner gnaw our arms off than miss—and later that night, after innumerable shots of bourbon, freeze us at The High Hat with a panoramic gaze across the table and a mumbled monologue in what I would have sworn was Swedish.

It was because I was drawn to him and because he didn't have time for me that I began to see more of Sarah. I'd visit with her at the bookstore where she worked and I'd listen, at the house, while she practiced her cello. We'd talk about Les. He was our narcotic.

* * *

Maybe I fell in love with Les through Sarah, but what it looked like to some people was that I had fallen in love with her. Maybe I had fallen in love with Sarah too, somehow, but I couldn't really tell where Les stopped and she began. They were so entangled, you couldn't razor them apart.

Even when she was complaining about Les to me, she spoke about him with a kind of violent intensity spiked with awe. As though he were a god with some regrettably tragic underworld habits.

I began to speak badly of him at the same time that it must have been obvious that I was aping his gestures and certain phrases he used. *Vice versa* became *verse visa*. Instead of *as usual*, I'd say *per usual*. So and so is *excellent company*, I'd mimic. Or, *Yeah, he's good news*. Or I'd add Les's familiar *as they say* to my own sentences. *Gotta go, as they say*. I wanted him to disappear so I could become him.

Because it was said he'd earned a black belt and made money for a while in Mountain Home by teaching karate to police officers, I studied karate from a book I bought at the bookstore where Sarah worked. At night, in the window of my apartment over the Laundromat, I kicked at my reflection, hissing.

29

* * *

Having quit surveying for the day, we fell together, *per usual*, at The High Hat before heading home. Quinton, Les, me, and now and then two part-timers, Mike and Brady. A traveling fair was encamped outside town and several of the carnies stood at the bar, lumped together and awkward like remnants of some outcast race. Three about our age and one considerably more weathered. Maybe a full set of teeth between them. Out of place not so much for what they wore, although the fat one's t-shirt didn't cover his stomach, but for the way their movements were out of sync. Their heads bobbled around on their necks like windshield figurines and their voices were ill-tuned to the bar's low-key hum.

Before we finished our beers, Les kicked up from the booth, mug in hand. In a subdued voice, as though talking to himself, he said, I should be with them. And he walked over to them and said something and they closed in around him like brothers and when I left, soon after that, I couldn't even catch his eye to nod goodnight.

* * *

When people saw Les, they touched him. Coming into the bar or into the surveyor's office before work, he would pass through a gauntlet of hands extended in greeting. He was like a votive stone. For his own part, he was reserved. But men and women alike, cursory acquaintances and friends, hugged him hello and goodbye or touched him on the shoulder, people who saw him every day, people who weren't physical with anyone else.

I was desperate for him to notice me, to like me. But I had nothing to offer someone like him. My adoration was worthless. He had awakened in me something major, life-changing. An imagination of a different way to be in the world. He was determined and he was at ease inside his body. You looked at him, at the loose way he walked, and you thought about sex. His torso rode on his hips like a snake on its coil. Maybe he wasn't even fully conscious of the effect he had on me. But part of what he awakened in me was a horrible awareness that I would never be the only person I now wanted to be.

* * *

He invited me to spend a Saturday hiking through Lost Valley with him and Sarah. It was all I wanted, my two infatuations on either side of me. The day was a stunner. The bright purplish-red flowers of Judas trees lit up the north-facing slope, glittering in a pointillist blur of oaks and maples and shagbark hickories. But at the beginning of the dirt path that only accommodated two side by side, Les and Sarah began talking about François Villon. Very earnestly, as if it were going to affect the way they conducted the rest of their lives. And for nearly an hour I followed them morosely and they didn't think to include me, even out of politeness. They didn't throw me a crust of the conversation. We passed a huge wild black cherry tree they never noticed and when we reached the peak, I wandered off so they'd be forced to come looking for me, which they did, irritably, as though I were the asshole, before we started back down in silence.

* * *

The first time I saw him naked, we had been surveying near Bull Shoals Lake and Sarah met us at the boathouse with three tickets to see Bobby Bland's second set at The Palace. We packed our gear into Quinton's truck and borrowed his flashlight. Quinton said *hasta luego* and drove back to town. And then we went down to the dock, Sarah leading with the flashlight in case a moccasin had curled onto the still-warm planks. She stripped first and I will never forget the luminescence of her angular body in the semi-dark. The long line of her clavicles and her extended throat and the breathtaking slight swing of her breasts as she bent to sit and then slid off the mossy edge of the dock into the water.

I could smell him when he took off his shirt— vinegar and goat. His muscled arms and stocky legs. He shucked his jeans and boxers in one motion and dove from the dock quickly but not before I glimpsed and then—as right in front of me his body jackknifed open over waves lit softly by the full moon—clearly saw a leather ring around his cock and balls.

* * *

Les answered the door after I knocked on a weekday after midnight. I had been drinking Wild Turkey with Quinton and felt shattered. I needed to see Les because he eclipsed me. I despised him, I was in love with him. I coveted Sarah's consuming, inflamed, total love for him. I knew I would never have the means to elicit that kind of devotion from anyone.

So I found myself parked in front of their house and then at their door, drunk, weeping, ridiculous, sucking in big quavery breaths. And he stepped outside with me into the yard so we wouldn't wake Sarah, his thick hair mussed with sleep, and he listened to me crying and blubbering about my last girlfriend. Stood there in boxer shorts and a white undershirt with his arms across his chest and it started to rain but he didn't move and I kept on blubbering but I was aware too of the rain and cold and I felt less sure about why I was so upset and he stood there listening to me even after the conviction of emotion washed out of my voice. I was thinking we ought to go inside because it was pouring and the rain was like ice, but he didn't seem to notice and he was present for my benefit, tuned to me without offering any facile analysis or palliative.

There was a pause and then just the sound of the rain beating the grass and a whooshing like ocean around us in the leafy oaks. Then the light in the living room came on and I glanced at the window but didn't see Sarah and he never took his eyes off my face. At once I knew I didn't believe the things I was saying, that I hadn't come to their door in pangs of grief for my old girlfriend but for other reasons entirely. Again, I glanced at the window and wanted to go inside. I imagined being inside looking out at us in the rain, the wide, relaxed shoulders of the poet blocking out a clear view of me. I started shivering and my words guttered out. All that magmatic emotion had subsided. I felt nothing but cold and wet and I wanted to go inside to be with them.

Then he said something to me—I no longer remember what—and I stepped forward with anxiety and relief and hugged him, but he was distant, his body solid and stiff, my ear pressed briefly to his hard shoulder, to the wet transparentized cloth over his skin.

* * *

Les, in the truck bed, handed me the prism pole and I stood it straight up next to the pickup and checked the bull's-eye bubble to see that I had it vertical and plumb. Les strapped the meter box to his back and jumped to the ground. Then he put the tripod over his right shoulder and picked up the theodolite. The hair around the back of his neck was already wet and he set down the tripod and wiped it all to one side.

I'll take the theodolite, I offered.

Alright.

Someone started up a lawnmower. I snapped the hammer into its holster on my belt and patted my shirt pocket to feel my pencil. With my left hand, I balanced the prism pole which, with swaths of pink surveying tape tied to it, looked something like an Indian lance. The equipment was fairly heavy. Following Les across the parking lot, I was taking inventory. I could feel the measuring tape in my front pocket and the knife in its leather casing tapping against my thigh. All set.

Got your two-way? Les asked, not looking back.

Yep. Field book?

He tapped his breast pocket.

I loved these times when the two of us were sent out together. I loved watching him, feeling my own neck and shoulders make little sympathetic adjustments to the way he moved. It didn't matter whether he was walking into a room full of people or leaning into the transit in the middle of a field, he was more hypnotic than anyone I'd ever seen. It was a strange electric quality like when leaves take on the first shimmer of color in the fall. And maybe it was his death in him, pressing early to the surface of his skin, that gave him some kind of radiance. There was something purely erotic about it. And when we surveyed, whether he was speaking to me through the two-way or calling out matter of fact questions and numbers, I felt an almost masochistic charge, an undercurrent of throbbing obedience to him that weakened the sockets behind my knees and sometimes gave me inconvenient hard-ons.

Two nuthatches were chasing each other around the scaley bark of a bull pine. Les pulled out the legs of the tripod and clamped the distance meter to it. He looped the battery cord over the adjustment screw. I checked my pockets for flagging as I walked over to the control point between two laurel bushes and turned the prism pole reflector toward Les.

What's your height, Les called.

This is seven-four.

OK. Let's backsight and get going.

For the rest of the morning, I shouted to Les a description of each shot—*Flow line of curb, Toe of slope, Building corner*—which he'd write into the field book next to the shot readings. I drew the lines of each shot across my field sketch. Then, when I could see Les push the EDM's battery-off button and start to record his readings, I'd move on to the next shot.

The temperature rose quickly and we were both as wet as if we'd been swimming in our clothes, but the work was all easy and in-tune.

That evening, it was stifling. As much for the air conditioning as anything, I went to Lana's Café and ate shepherd's pie and kale and then walked across the street to The High Hat for a beer. It was a little before sunset when Les came in and walked right up to me where I was sitting with a couple of fiddle players. He nodded at everyone and he bent down to tell me that he wanted to show me something. Alright, I said.

You're going to need to pay up. It's a ways from here.

Alright, I said.

We can take my truck.

His windows were up and I opened the passenger door, scooting into a coffin of baked air. My first breath seared the inside of my nostrils and heat from the seat radiated into my thighs and shoulder blades. The inside of the windshield was a mess of smeared mosquitoes.

We rolled down the windows in synch.

He drove down the hill and off the pavement onto a dirt road where the pharmacist lived. Tied to the barbwire fence, a half-dozen large catfish heads dangled like church bells. A whippoorwill was calling. In the fall and winter, I used to run along this road, and although there were only a few houses, there were a lot of dogs. I had my arm out the window. Fireflies lit up the hill by the pharmacist's house. The cab filled with dust. The road crossed a cow guard and wound upward. Les turned his headlights on and, a hundred yards later, pulled into the weeds where the road crossed a creek. Here it is, he said. Careful, it's slope-shouldered.

Woods on both sides.

I followed him into the woods, up the branch

through knee-high ferns. He kept telling me we had to hurry, we might be too late. We came to a little rise and a cairn of mossgrown rock. There's a little cave here, he said. We missed the bats already, but take a look at this.

The hole in the rock went straight down. It was only the diameter of a garbage can lid. I could make out something quivering along the lip of it, and when I stepped closer, I instinctively jumped back again and slipped on some lichens and fell to one knee. It's ok, it's ok, Les said softly. He wasn't talking to me, he was talking to the swarm of chestnut-size creatures exiting the mouth of the cave.

What the fuck *are* they? I heard myself whisper. I didn't want them to notice me if they hadn't already. My jeans were torn and my knee throbbed where I'd cut it on the rock.

Some kind of giant cricket, I guess, he whispered back. No kind I've ever seen before.

* * *

In the window booth of The High Hat one night, Quinton and I were drinking drafts when Les came in and wound his way over to our table. He was talking in a strange, quiet patois. I kept asking, What, what, what, and he kept on, his voice animated and his eyes half-closed, almost reptilian, but I had no idea what he was saying, not even what language it was, not even whether it was a language. After he downed a beer, he got quiet and then left.

What was that? I asked Quinton.

Yeah, oh well, when he's drunk he'll talk like that now and again. Picked it up one weekend in New Orleans.

Quinton and I stayed until just before closing when Quinton started to look queasy. He stood up like he'd been bit and glanced toward the men's room and then he looked toward the door to the street. The street was closer. The High Hat was packed and a lot of people were dancing. Quinton started away without saying anything to me, his cheeks starting to puff and blow, as though he were struggling with some conundrum. I saw him pause by a table where no one was sitting, kneel on one knee like a knight, pick up a woman's purse from the floor, open it, and puke into it in one gushing heave. Then he propped the purse up against the table leg and stood, wiping his face, adjusting his ponytail. And he went on out through the door.

* * *

By lunch break, we were near Jasper so we went for a swim in the Buffalo River near the bridge. There were some picnicking families there too. Les dove off the bluff a couple times and swam over to the shore where I was soaking in the sun. Just downstream from me, on the sand, there were half a dozen bluegill heads swarming with bluebottle flies. Les approached the woman in shorts and an orange tank top who had been calling her son out of the water, but he spoke to the boy. Lars, Les said, you're probably the only Lars in Arkansas. The boy didn't answer anything, but his mother, wrapping a towel around him, said, We named him Lars because my family's Dutch.

I had already put on my boots, and I came over to tell Les that everyone else was waiting by the trucks. Les said, But isn't Lars a Swedish name?

Yeah, yeah, the woman said sharply, but Americans don't know the difference. With her hand on his shoulder, she began to direct the boy toward the campsite.

A quick movement in Les's face as he glanced back at me—I wasn't even sure he had seen me coming up behind him—kept me from wise-cracking, and then, even before I realized what stopped me, Les released my eyes with an expression as subtle as a watermark.

Take care, Lars, he called after the boy.

* * *

I came into The High Hat and they invited me over—Sarah and Les and some young filmmaker from out of state who had read Les's books and was shooting a film based on interviews with him and images from the poems. The air smelled like stale beer and dirty laundry. They were salting the foam on their draft beers. The filmmaker's name—Bill or John, I don't recall now. And as soon as I was seated and before I could order a beer, they leaned forward again as though their faces pressed some invisible concern between them, and they began again to talk, Les in his slow smoked-ham of a voice and the filmmaker, Bill or John, interjecting little riffs of counterpoint, and Sarah animated, nodding her head. The waitress didn't come over to ask what I wanted to drink. No one at the table made an effort to bring me into the conversation, and I couldn't follow it.

Now Les was saying that to be defiled—was that what he said?—was to become recognizable to yourself. Which sounded to me like priceless garbage. I couldn't piece together his argument, if that's what it was. My mind hung on phrases— dumb abundance, crushed stones, the colors in Giotto's paintings. Letting one space tell against another. It was all over the place.

It would have been humiliating to stand up and go to the bar while Les talked because the talk was so clearly a process for him, or an intricate pretense, of thinking something through. Also, I wanted to be among them, part of the conversation. But I couldn't add anything and because I couldn't either excuse myself or sip a beer I didn't have, I kept watching the three of them, though mostly Les, with ratcheting unease. I focused on his facial movements as though they might be more decipherable than his words. I noted the way he tented and untented his hands in front of his mouth and I stifled my panic with reminders that I wasn't stupid, I'd come late to a discussion already in progress, I was suffering the fatigue of four straight days surveying in the sun, and they probably had read things or seen movies that provided a context I didn't share.

But I was stranded there for twenty or thirty long minutes. Caught by that root indetermination from which, I could suddenly see it was true, all the events of my life have stretched out.

I had come to the table happy to see Les, buoyant, with a slight self-conscious swagger that I liked to think characterized me, and with every intention of paying for the next round. Without any doubt I would have something to say. But I was forever unqualitied by Les. Emptied out. He had some kind of juju that turned me into a manikin. At best, I was wounded by every encounter with him. And I began to think, leaning my elbows on the table, looking from his face to Sarah's, that I would only heal if he were harmed.

* * *

We had gotten high and hungry and we stopped on our way back from a party in Fayetteville for which all the guests, to gain entry, needed to be dressed as a character from a Dylan song. Les, invited by a professor he knew, hadn't planned to go. But after he told us about it at work, we harassed him until he promised to take us.

We met up in the parking lot by the office.

Quinton, reeking of Brut and high on crank, was dressed as always in jeans, t-shirt, and Stetson, but he had a thick, filthy rope he'd taken from a construction site. This he had spray-painted a patchy blue and wrapped around his torso and shoulder like a boa constrictor. He was squatting and offering an unlit cigarette to a bedraggled beagle that had wandered over and he was talking obsessively to Les about college pussy.

Les had on a safari suit he'd bought at an auction in the winter and he wore the white pants and vest with a mismatched jacket so torn up it looked like it might have been used to train police dogs. And he had a child's plastic tiara wrapped with some loose rushes wedged on his head.

I was dressed in overalls and a straw hat, my pockets stuffed with nickels I was planning to pass out to people who couldn't guess who I was.

But as soon as we arrived, I gave it away by asking the guy at the door, who was dressed evidently as a string bean, if he was having a good time. He said, Maggie's brother, right? He looked over Les and Quinton. Napoleon in rags and Tangled Up in Blue, but Tangled Up in Blue's not a character.

Yeah look who's talking, fucking green bean, Quinton blurted as he pushed inside, Les and I falling in behind him.

We started back to Eureka Springs after midnight and passed a Mr. Burger that was still open. We looked at each other and Les started laughing that infectious, ridiculous laugh of his and we were all laughing. Les had a hard time parking his truck. We stepped inside like a travesty of the three kings, Quinton so drunk and high his eyes were almost shut and his mouth hung open. I felt every face swerve toward us and I smiled at the girl taking my order. Heard myself laugh a little fake laugh that indicated to her that I knew I looked like an idiot, but I was just pretending to be an idiot, I wasn't really an idiot, and she grinned back to let me know she suspected as much. But Les stepped up after me in that bizarre costume and ordered his quarter pounder with cheese. He straight-faced it right through. And no one smirked.

I could see it was a kind of exercise for him. He couldn't let anything fall away from his control, any aspect of himself. It wasn't any concern for dignity, which he could have salvaged just as I did, smiling and nodding. It was a matter of who would control the material. Les took control. And of course his doing so was an accusation and a verdict on how I had handled myself. I had blinked, so to speak. I'd let them make me look obsequious. For the sake of appearance. We'd arrived at a fork and I'd gone one way and he didn't respect me enough to follow. Instead, he'd presumed to add up all the reasons I might have had for choosing my direction. Then, he crossed them out one by one. He'd disregarded my reasoning, my moral character, our camaraderie, even my dumb luck to be first in line.

And it all reversed. Envy turned me inside out. I hated him. While he stood with his fingertips drumming the counter by the register, I felt like I could smell his death rise up in him, flush with the veins and scars on his forearms, plumb with the rise of his cheekbones and the dense bright gaze of his eyes. I felt I suddenly had power because he didn't suspect me. I could get inside him without him knowing it, like a parasite.

* * *

Heading back, we trudged through thickets of liana and berry brambles close to the river's edge in sweaty jeans and long sleeves despite the heat, all of us reeking of Off. Quinton was pissed and he was swinging the machete even when he didn't need to. I saw him cleave a yellow butterfly in flight.

When we left the water, we climbed through shortleaf pines until we came out onto a bluff, everybody silent, me and the two part-timers closing in around Quinton. Below us, the river gleamed, its surface stippled with breezes. In the clear green water, I could make out big chert blocks that had loosened from the bluff and plunged into the shallows. The sun glinted from our two-ways and from the prism pole in my hand. When we moved again, a covey of quail exploded from the bushes next to us. My heart jumped as they veered across the river, the pant of their wings quickly diminishing.

We came back to the river one more time near a stand of old cottonwoods whose gnarly bark had been rubbed smooth, chest high, by elk. Quinton lowered his machete.

It's all spider web from here, he said. You earned it, Clay. You lead.

He handed me the machete.

I hated spider webs. I hated all of it. The sac spiders and deer ticks and poison caterpillars and clouds of mosquitoes and chiggers running around my fingers and rattlesnakes and eye gnats. But I had fucked up the job, the numbers didn't work out and the lines didn't close. It wasn't even supposed to be my job. I was filling in for Les who had called in supposedly sick. I'd volunteered and now I had to ride the fucking beef.

Even with the canoes hoisted onto the racks in the pickup, the orange theodolite and station cases and wet bundles packed away, with everybody pulling warm Cokes out of the cooler and Quinton preening his belly-hair for ticks with the silent absorption of a gorilla, there wasn't any feeling of deliverance or satisfaction. Not only were we going to have to come back out here, but I knew that Quinton would have me putting in overtime after that.

If Les hadda been here, Quinton started. He didn't finish the sentence.

I hawked and spat and turned away and pulled myself into the truck bed under the canoes.

* * *

With our work boots tracking little hexes of dried mud behind us, we trudged into Lana's Café in the same order we'd walked most of the day, Quinton, me, and the two part-timers, Brady and Mike.

Brenda came over with four bottles of Budweiser. Usual? she asked. Or you want to see the menu?

Quinton was wagging his thumbnail across the bristles of his chin and looking at the door as though the act of speaking hadn't caught up with him yet. The air conditioning hummed, but it was still warm and humid inside.

I ordered the special and got up to take a leak, passing the pay phone on the way to the men's room. When I came out again, I walked straight to the register where Brenda was cashiering someone out. I took the fifty-dollar bill I always carry in my wallet—considered for a brief moment the weed I wasn't going to be able to buy now—and asked Brenda for change.

Without turning, she reached behind her and wiped her fingers against the condensation at the side of the ice cooler. Then she counted out my change.

Four tens a five and five ones? she asked.

How about you keep it all and do me a favor.

Her eyes dilated and she tilted her face to the side, half flirtatious, half suspicious.

Depends, she smiled.

Here's the thing, I said. Just next time Les comes in, it might take a couple tries, see if you can make out the number he calls when he uses the phone.

She looked over my shoulder at someone who must have raised an arm for her attention.

How am I supposed to do that? She sounded disappointed.

I don't know. That's why I'm giving you fifty bucks. Go to the bathroom or something when you see him pick up the phone.

I took a mint patty from the bowl on the counter and turned back to the table and she didn't say anything special to me or treat me any differently for two weeks, although I was there almost every other night, sometimes alone, sometimes with Quinton and Les and others.

It was clear to me that Les could only hold his multiple lives in suspension for so long.

On Friday, the end of June, I went up to the counter and paid. And Brenda called my name as I was turning for the door.

Got something for you, she said.

* * *

Working alone on Sunday, I walked back to the truck, put a foot on the bumper, and pulled myself over the tailgate. I squatted by a broken bundle of pantile lath and rummaged around through the toolbox. I took out a Phillips head, climbed down, and unscrewed one of the reflectors on Quinton's tailgate. I swiped the grime against my army pants and went over to the tri-station at the curb and propped the reflector on a stone. Then I walked back toward the truck where the transit was set up, the electronic distance-meter clamped to it. Squinting through the sight at the reflector, I started to adjust the mirror for light and I fiddled with the fine-tuning knobs and the locks. Finally, I shot the distance, took the read-out, and pulled the field book from my front pants pocket. A couple of nails fell out—a long one for dirt and two short concrete nails—and I bent to pick them up and slipped them back into my pocket. I recorded the distance in the field book. After that, I recorded the zenith angle. Something the size of a sparrow came flying out of nowhere and hit against my shoulder and clung there. I stood still, slowly turning my head to look at the praying mantis. The praying mantis raised the axes of her arms and swiveled her head and seemed, with both of those stalked grape-shot eyes, to look me fully in the face.

* * *

What happened wasn't engineered, never is. What happens always does when I'm not paying attention, when I'm looking at my shoelaces, taking a dump, when I've let my guard down. It's as if every time I start to do something I've planned for months, I get hit in the back of the head with a bottle someone chucks from a passing van. And I abandon whatever it was I meant to do, I'm already in motion, I'm doing something else, just reacting, and whatever I planned is payed out way behind me.

* * *

Quinton was putting the equipment in the truck on Monday morning. I slipped into his private room and made a long distance phone call on his office phone. Then I bolted out into the summer heat almost trembling. I didn't want Quinton to catch me on his phone and I was already pricked by a sense of menace and malaise. I left behind my cap and the can of Off.

By late morning, sweat darkened Quinton's t-shirt in huge patches. The backpack straps were gnawing my shoulders. We walked through a pasture surrounded by forest, picking ticks from our arms, an orb of gnats over our heads. Quinton wore his Stetson, which drew the gnats up above his face, but I was having to swipe at the air every few steps. I kept my lips tight, but the gnats crawled up my nose and I could feel them clotting the back of my throat. We worked for most of three hours without speaking much. The phone call I'd made kept replaying in my mind, the gnats were glomming to the corners of my eyes and I couldn't stay focused.

Quinton would forget to use the two-way and resort to shouting, motioning with one hand while he aimed the gun and took his reading.

Left, left. No! YOUR left! Wake up! Left a hair, left a hair. Left some more. Left, left.

A killdeer circled, its *dee-ee* rising. A plane droned, invisible. I was a good sixty yards away from Quinton in green fescue. There were milk-weed plants here and there and I knew they would ruin the hay—it's toxic to horses. But it wasn't my problem.

Step out the way of the pole, Quinton called. The point's about two feet toward me.

When we toggled up to the next site, I set up the theodolite and tightened the leg screws. I stepped on each of the tripod's feet to dig the points into the soft dirt, and I sighted down to the nail and set the angle, trying to stay on task. Quinton was consulting his notes and punching numbers into the data collector. The phone call I'd made was still looping in my head. I kept adding things I might have said, changing my tone, making it more and less succinct. I picked up the bag and started down the slope toward the barbwire fence. Then I went back for the prism pole.

The peninsula of pasture we were in was most-ly surrounded by oak forest.

I dropped the bag over the barbwire fence and

rested the pole against the wire on the other side. In the splintered knots of the fence post, I could see swatches of brown and colorless fur. Deer or—more likely—cattle. I took a few more steps and the trees closed around me.

Quinton's voice crackled over the two-way. What's it look like out there?

Can't see you, I answered.

Some shot. We'll have to hack through to each other. Is it all briars there?

Not really.

A minute passed. Then the two-way crackled again. Yeah, that looks OK for a line, Quinton was saying. Give me a wave. I'm trying to focus on you. Keep waving. Whoa. Right a hair. Right, right, right. Face it the other way. Left a hair. Ho!

I couldn't hear the gun beep, but I knew it had and that Quinton was punching in the horizontal distance. I waited, wondering what would come of my phone call. I kept pulling my eyelid down over the bottom lip of my eye to try to strain out a gnat that felt big as an acorn, but my fingers were filthy and I couldn't dislodge it.

Point's fifteen feet away, Quinton's voice said. Can you get it from seventy-nine? What kind of boot was that?

I lowered the prism pole and unhooked the two-way from my back pocket again. Four feet, I said into it. No, four feet six. I can see seventy-nine perfect from here.

OK. We'll set em both from seventy-nine. Hang there for a second.

I laid down the prism pole beside a tree and fitted the two-way back on my belt, and I bent over the bag to get my machete. I was in a semi-clearing in the forest, but it was growing in. My eye was killing me. The machete blade, which had been spray-painted neon pink at one time, was rusty on both edges. I swung it flat-bladed at the gnats. Then I cut some of the vines around the witness stake, jammed the machete into the dirt and went back to rubbing my eye. The two-way was silent. The phone call in my head, phrases standing out. Not much of a conversation really. I looked at the filth around my fingernails and then at the hairs curling from a poison ivy vine. For a while, I closed my bad eye and with the other I watched the yellow horseshoe shape on the back of a tick crawling up my sleeve.

* * *

I set it in motion with the phone call. Telling myself I was doing it for Sarah's sake. Even for Les's sake. A beautiful scorpion, righteousness. I had no way to know what would happen. Les was cheating on his wife by living with Sarah. He was cheating on Sarah every weekend he spent with his wife. He cheated on both of them the afternoons and mornings and evenings he cut corners at work to meet the bartender, the guitar player, the potter, and whatever others there were. Of course, he never had time for me.

I called his wife. Surprised no one else had done it. Les was in New Orleans visiting his mother. Called Cora at her farm in Missouri from Quinton's office before work. I'm calling with bad news, like they say. Can't tell you who this is. Then I explained to Cora about Les and his so-called lesbian roommate, Sarah. Cora was in Eureka Springs that evening, knocking on Sarah's door. The next day, Sarah called in sick at the bookstore. I dropped by the bookstore and then the Owen Street house, but no one would answer the door.

If the three of them had made it through the next night, when Les got back from New Orleans, it could have gone differently. If they had made it through the night, some sort of resolutions might have been hammered out. There might have been a future. Forgiveness.

There might have been a future and forgiveness even for me.

Cora had showed up at Sarah's door. They'd talked. Around midnight, they called Les in New Orleans. Sarah called. Hi Les, guess who's here at the house?

So he hauled his excellent company back to Eureka Springs at once, but its excellence was gone flat. Sarah told me about it once in the nightmarish weeks afterwards, and I didn't ask again. The three of them together for the first time. The vomiting and screaming in the kitchen. Cora kneeing him in the balls. And Les staying quiet through it all, as though he had already transformed. An almost ceramic glaze to his eyes. A hideous night of lies springing undone. And towards morning, he asked Cora and Sarah if he could rest for a little. And the door to the bedroom closed and then the two women heard a gunshot. Three gunshots. And Cora ran out of Sarah's house screaming.

* * *

It's a barren feeling to know at the age of twenty five that you've already lived the most intense period of your life, that a vividness has blazed up and short-circuited something in you and you will remember what it felt like to be alive but not feel it again, and you won't even want to remember, can't bear it, it's too ploughed with guilt and pain. It seemed all of a sudden like a wind had slacked off and I was left leaning off-balance in a world something considerable had passed through. Once I had choices. Then it was as if my life leaped out of my body.

Sarah:
Beyond This Point, Monsters

The first man I went down on. You tasted like well water.

When you walked through doors, otherwise graceful as a mink, you invariably banged one shoulder against the frame. No explanation.

Here it says that hair cells in the ear convert sound waves to electrical signals.

It's lifting the end of its phrases. Not a veery. A gray-cheeked thrush I'd bet anything, but we won't see it.

Bushes scandent with white berries.

It was a simple question. I would have answered right away. But you considered it, dragging the cuticle of your thumbnail over your chapped lips, staring at the saltshaker on the table. Finding the full potential of the words. Making of it a larger question.

So you rescued us from the commonplace. Coaxed out the best in us. Which was your great gift.

When you opened my shirt, you stepped back and said, *They must envy each other.*

The Jammed Log Position.

How you made me laugh. I couldn't have fallen in love with you otherwise.

Broken chevrons of dry mud on the kitchen linoleum. And over newspaper on the table, a heap of freshly picked green beans.

Fat green-backed fly, dead, on the lath of the kitchen window.

I guess you were what the tragedians would call my bosom snake.

When we heard Rahsaan Roland Kirk's recording *Bright Moments*, you told me that his producer was mostly deaf from childhood smallpox. A deaf producer recording a blind musician who was promoted by a famous radio station with the call letters WHAT.

I don't think poets tell things at all, you said. *Poetry listens.*

The greater the cilia vibration, the louder the sound.

I stepped outside again, wishing you home. In the driveway, something was glowing on the windshield of my car. A kind of design. As I came near, my hackles up, I could make out the shape of a heart you must have smeared on the windshield with a crushed lightning bug. I heard a sound and turned and you were standing at the door where I had been a moment before, watching me in the driveway in the dark.

Your ever-present moleskin notebooks. Even when you surveyed.

The red-bellied woodpecker swerves over the primroses and claps itself to the crab apple trunk as if a magnet had drawn it. In dreams, that's how I come to you.

October wind, carrying the sound of distance. And then a hush rippling through the trees.

You bought me nipple rouge. I mail-ordered you a leather cock ring. Your eyes erupted when you opened it.

The name. The name of my beloved.

Woke on the floor to find a line of ants trailing from the baseboard to the cut in my palm.

Not seeing the cup in the bathroom, you brought me a mouthful of water in your mouth.

Standing at the window, wrapped in a bed sheet, watching bats sip nectar from the clematis.

Sweetest was your imagination.

You said that the world must listen to living things the way Miles Davis listens to music, marking everything that might be left out.

When I came home from work, you were crumbling sage over rainbow trout. Except for eggs at breakfast, that was the first and last meal you made me. The idea of cooking you loved, but not cooking itself. You would go to Lana's Café and eat the same thing five nights in a row.

You stayed tuned to the orioles and warblers of mid-May. *First*, you said, *the bug-eaters, then the seed-eaters fly through.*

Trying to comprehend the mechanics of hearing, scientists measured ripples across the cochlea of dead dogs.

Your ears must still be registering sounds, Les. Underground.

The way your lips relax when you sleep. And you lose your face, and a boy lies in bed next to me.

Did I wake you? Was I kicking?

A can of linseed oil in the front closet where I made you keep your Red Wing boots.

Dust carving out interiors in the sky at sunset.

And was Coltrane really a pallbearer at Sydney Bechet's funeral in Paris?

Was that a lie too?

Good news, Les. You're pre-approved for a MasterCard.

Everything worthwhile in me. Cut out. I leave the house and feel even the trees bend away from my affliction.

The name of my beloved is Abyss.

You turned me on to François Villon who was an orphan like you. Who was, like you, schooled by monks. Villon, who killed a priest one night in a tavern because, he swore in court, the priest had blasphemed God.

Villon, that superb liar.

The subtlety of your visual attention. You could alert me or change the subject with a contraction of your iris.

Almost after you've walked past it, snagging the dirty Kleenex from the table and bending down, without slowing, to pick up a dead spider I noticed days ago and meant to sweep up and then forgot. That economy of your gestures. The multiplying purpose.

Natural strategist.

Love solves nothing, but your love made me appear to myself.

Remember when I was lying on your lap and you cleaned my ears with a Q-tip? What a strange, complex intimacy, your at once maternal and sexual tenderness.

The Transverse Lute Position.

Leon Thomas with Oliver Nelson in Berlin, yodeling through "Straight No Chaser."

For the filmmaker, you took off your clothes and stretched out at the lake shore where the murky water lapped your side. Your eyes closed. Gorgeous drowned man. Practicing.

You would quote Thoreau on the wood thrush: "Whenever a man hears it . . . the gates of heaven are not shut against him."

Each complex tone, a superposition of pure tones.

I remember discovering that you loved to have your eyebrows stroked. That was a novel sensation to me, stroking a man's eyebrows. Somehow, it had never occurred to me.

You do not age. Someone else will watch me grow old.

I walk, invisibly mutilated, toward the mirror.

Whether I stand or sit or drive to the grocery, it seems I only stake out an incoherence.

The amethystine blue of your eyes, you said once.

I wake each morning exhausted.

If only routine would brush sensation aside.

Then there are doves cooing.

And I am still here.

Innumerable others

have survived much worse.

There are many events worse than a single death. Who am I

to stop going forward? To not even want to heal?

To fail to draw the skin over this wound.

But if to go on is to go without.

I a wraith.

If you don't live it, Charlie Parker swore, it won't come out of your horn.

Live what?

In the corner of the door jamb, the spider flings legfuls of web over the moth, spinning it around like a chunk of wood on a lathe. Who do you think I'm thinking of, Les?

I moved your chair and look! Two popcorn kernels that must have fallen from your lap the week before you died.

My encounter with what has been kept in store for me began the night you shut your breath off.

True love, wrote Walter Raleigh, is a durable fire in mind.

But how can I find you in that stupendous blaze?

Hanging between two nails in the garage, your Eagle Claw rod with its Shakespeare Alpha spinning reel. On another nail, the unopened package of thirty pound test Trilene line I gave you at Christmas.

François Villon, born in the year they burned Joan of Arc. You loved the poems Villon wrote for his friends in underworld slang.

Green, empty beer bottles glittering in the weeds and chicory beside the driveway.

Come here, you whispered, pulling me through the back door. *I was raking leaves from the raspberries and found a nest of spring salamanders.*

Your orange Off can under the bathroom sink. Even the memory of the smell immobilizes me. A surveyor's cologne.

When I noticed the shrew quivering beside the garbage can by the driveway, I thought it was injured. I bent close before I saw it was dead, shaken by beetles devouring it from underneath. And I vomited beside it.

You not here to blame, I blame myself. You not here to flay, I flay myself.

Face in the mirror crumpled by grief.

Yeah, but listen *to what Stein is saying: a rose is eros is a rose is eros.*

Sweetest was your intimate impulse.

The twenty minutes and fifty seconds of "Harvest Time" on Pharoah Sanders's album *Pharoah*. Spare broken chords, intensely felt cropped lines, and those emotional halts before his finishing phrases.

Pharoah. Born Farrell Sanders, just outside Little Rock.

When a sound wave enters the inner ear, cilia all along the cochlea's length vibrate.

He's excellent company, you would say about someone you liked. *He's serious good news.*

For my birthday you gave me a stick with the dry foam cloud of a praying mantis egg sack attached to it.

At ease in honesty, you praised me: *very rare.*

What bothers me, I told you in the first weeks after we met, is that I never know when you think I'm interesting.

Now, you said. *When you say things like that.*

The empty nail in the wall by the back door where you hung your tattered duck-cloth jacket.

I'm reading about a woman who, before she was taken captive by Pawnees, managed to hide her baby under a bush near her house. When she returned from captivity, she found its bones there.

Your marriage was over, you told me. Over. *It went dead in the bed.*

The silence of the house has intensified. What woke me last night were snails scraping up the window glass.

The Fetching Fire Behind the Hill Position.

We penciled our silhouettes on the bedroom wall by candlelight. Holding the candle, you drew me lying on my back—forehead, nose, chin, collarbone, breast, nipple. And then I traced your silhouette, not facing mine, as you wanted, but also on your back, merged with mine. A double landscape. Inside each other.

Where are those conversations that awed me, that made me howl? Now when only they could save me.

I'm gagging on the hours.

When Cora came to the house, the night before you died, she forced her way into the bedroom. When she saw the silhouettes, her face uncolored. I knew you'd done the same thing with her, that in her own bedroom your candle-lit silhouette and hers were merged on the wall.

Your marriage wasn't over. Over. Wasn't *dead in the bed*. Was it?

In every photograph, your soul has exited from your face.

What's wrong with me that I trusted you. What's wrong with me that I didn't save you. That I was so lost, I didn't see what was happening. Didn't stop you. I made you think I despised you. In your last hours on earth I spewed contempt on you. How could you not know it would pass? That my hatred was only a form of relief to have the truth out. And you didn't even grant me that. You snatched it away. You jammed your guilt so far down my throat it became my own and when will I stop suffocating on it?

The obscenity of hair in the brush buried in your drawer in the bathroom cabinet.

Bésame mucho. You laughed, *It doesn't just mean kiss.*

Stubbing your shoulder against the door frame.

I fatally opened myself on a poem. You are its name.

To say that after you died, I kept breathing. That weeks went by, that I ate meals, looked at a newspaper, slept in a bed with my head on the pillow. That I smiled at someone responsively. That I acted *as though.*

Just past breakfast, a week after my birthday, the mantis nymphs came out in a frenzy, hundreds of them, scrambling across the porch rail, stalking and eating each other. *Mantes,* you said when I called you to see, *you probably know it's the Greek word for prophet. And what's the prophecy? The world begins and ends in violence.*

On TV, footage of the refugees pushed back out to sea in their tawdry boat. What would you say, Les?

I notice the left rear tire of your truck losing air

in the driveway and rage reddens my face like a niacin rush.

Contrary to what they tell me, my return to ordinary life is neither stepwise nor slow. There is no return.

Can you see how the primroses have grown through the fence?

Sweetest was the kissing.

Who by fire, who by water, you by your own hand.

To get out of the house, I sat in the backyard yesterday, wearing sandals and sunglasses. Drank tequila and read your poems. Now the tops of my feet are striped with burn. The inside of me striped with burn.

Bitches Brew, Miles Davis. You loved the subtle changes in his dynamics.

When I practice the cello, I listen to what I can leave out.

The first time I heard you talk, I thought: he is speaking about *my* feelings, he is speaking in *my* stead, he knows everything.

They say the South American ghost eel makes a high-pitched piercing hum. Sometimes, it seems like the air around me must be full of them. Invisible. Screaming.

In your underwear drawer, I found an uncut geode. Everything means something, what does this mean? A memento? A present for someone? For me?

That first morning when you slept in my bed, I woke before you. And waking was the climax denied me all night.

You came back with honeysuckle from the mailbox post, pinched off the ends, and put two, a dark yellow and a white blossom, in each of our coffee cups. *Cuts the bitterness*, you smiled.

What made you think you could be left out?

The things you did dazzled me. But you shared them with others. The things you did dazzled others. But you shared them with me.

You open your hand and satisfy desire. I read that in Psalms and thought of you. Your long middle finger.

The yard's gone Mondrian with primroses, you said.

The Goat and Tree Position.

The old men are snag fishing for gar at the lake again.

When I compare the gloom inside the house with the darkness outside it, I find a way to simplify myself.

"Seven Steps to Heaven," Miles Davis.

Time is what the stars shine through.

And the brain determines pitch by the stimulated hair cells.

His hispidulous chin?! Is that what you said? That's not a word, try again.

It humps its wings like that when it feels threatened.

The rest of us made you the point where our astonishments and our projections converged.

On your desk: a fossil ammonite, tobacco-colored ink, a fountain pen, a shriveled walnut you compared once to an angel's scrotum.

Whoa. Not an owl, Horned Owl. Back up. Real slow.

Let me tell you about life without you.

The sound of leaves falling down through leaves. A night jar tongue-clicking while I'm too exhausted to sleep.

"Time After Time," Miles Davis. The spare broken chords make a kind of floating echo effect.

Just after you died, I missed my period.

Glair. That's whipped egg white. They used it as a binder for illuminated manuscripts. To get the right froth, Blake probably squeezed egg white in and out of a sponge for an hour.

I thought I was pregnant.

That you'd bequeathed me your baby.

But it was grief. Only that.

Try again.

Is that Hamlet holding up your skull?

The purple finch rubbing an ant along its outer primaries, from wrist to tip.

The bushes scandent with white berries.

My last birthday. The living room unlit. I suspected a surprise, but before I could reach the light switch, you struck a match to the horse skull you'd hung from the ceiling and doused with lighter fluid. It was the most beautiful thing I ever saw. The slow liquid-blue flame in the shape of a horse's skull flowering into a new dimension, turning slowly on a string in the dark.

I have been sitting here in a corner of The High Hat for hours like a blind dog. No one is coming to lead me away. I don't want to drink. I push a ten-dollar bill to the corner of the table so I can continue to sit.

The light moves away from me.

You bastard, you fucking bastard, how could you quit and leave me like this, rotting in my drool and incapacity, like a flap of cardboard in a swamp.

Webworms have gauzed our cherry tree.

It doesn't only *mean kiss me a lot*, you laughed.

Sweetest Les. Damaged Les.

I hit my brakes the instant I saw the raccoon.

But I couldn't stop the car.

Those eyes. Beyond panic.

The mirror on my bureau, I tilted it down.

Who in due time? Who before his time?

Half a dozen crows mobbing a red-tailed hawk. What kind of sign is that? What are you telling me?

Within ten minutes of meeting, we'd exchanged love letters from the corners of our eyes.

Desire, they say, is made of many desires. But my desires are made of one desire.

Whether opening the window lets more flies out or in.

Staring for an hour at crumbs in the seam of a book.

The hiss of the world against me.

Your moleskin notebooks. I can't bear to read them or put them away.

A thorn bug and her nymphs on the green stem.

Villon, who wrote his own epitaph as a ballad.

This one's filled with your neat, tiny handwritten notes on Coleridge.

At sunset the doves flock into our oaks and coo. They make so much noise,

the neighborhood dogs begin to howl.

When you were alive.

Under the shrew's body, the maggots were legion. The valves of their mouths opening and closing rapidly after the beetles scattered.

Was I kicking? Did I wake you?

Pharoah Sanders humming through the piccolo while he blows "Lower Egypt."

Itys, that's what you named the baby barn swallow under our porch eave.

How gently you would open and close the door not to alarm the mother bird.

And wouldn't let me turn on the porch light that spring.

The pizza delivery boy saying, I couldn't find your house.

Reaching for the little bottle of massage oil beside the bed, grabbing the wrong one

in the dark, you laved my clitoris with Tiger Balm.

Why Itys? I asked you.

I drape a scarf over the mirror so as not to see my face accidentally.

The sound, you said, serious, *it's the sound. When the mother returns to the nest, you hear her peeping Itys, Itys, Itys.*

I can no longer listen to Pharoah Sanders.

Can't sell the records.

Or give them away.

Or imagine anyone else listening to "Upper and Lower Egypt."

The hiss and pop: you in the kitchen frying eggs.

I dragged your record player to the basement. Brought it up again.

Bright Moments, Rahsaan Roland Kirk:
    Yes, yes.
    Bright moments.
    Bright moments is like hearing some music
        that ain't nobody else heard,
    and if they heard it they wouldn't even recog-
        nize that they heard it
    because they been hearing it all their life but
        they nutted on it,
    so when you hear it and you start popping
        your feet and jumping up and down
    they get mad because you're enjoying yourself
        but those are bright moments
    that they can't share with you
    because they don't know even how to go
        about listening to what you're listening
        to
    and when you try to tell them about it
    they don't know a damn thing about what
        you're talking about!

In the bucket of your mouth

you brought me water.

The lulling of doves.

Each day, your death's woven into fact and each
night, I let out the knots.

In bed, alone, in the dark, I fly toward you.

And through you.

This spring I see, dangling from the arborvitae, dozens of bagworm cocoons. Tiny mummies.

I'm glad you never watched the light in my eyes glint out.

The smoke blown away and then sucked back into the fire.

When breath meets the reed, the air propagates an elastic wave of energy.

Like the severed head of the egret we found by the path in the pine woods, its tangerine eye open, unclouded.

Was I kicking again?

Here it says that most people walk at least three hours every day to fetch water.

In the bucket of your mouth.

Villon: arrested a dozen times. He writes *The Testament* between jail stints. Then he's sentenced to the gallows. A last minute reprieve banishes him from Paris for ten years.

That was in 1463. Villon was thirty-four. No one saw him again.

So lightly you slept.

As though afraid to close the door

on consciousness. Were you afraid

of letting go?

You slept like a bird

with one tangerine eye open.

You nudged me awake

and said my name

when my legs kicked out.

Your long fingers on my stomach.

Itys, Itys, Itys.

Was I kicking? I thought I felt a baby kicking.

Beloved among women.

On Rifle Range Road the summer signs are up:
Tomatoes Corn Lopes Watermelon Queens.

They are fishing again from the overpass bridge.

When I drive back to our rent house

the primroses are gone.

Dead leaves blowing against the fence.

It was ages ago. Last year.

But whenever you went away, you always came back.

Not to be refused.

I sit lightly on the bed. To run my fingers through your curls.

Rubbing my tongue against prickles in back of my throat. I know I have a cold coming on.

So many hawks in the trees along the highway. You'd love their white breasts blazing in the sunset.

But to whom do I write this

if you are not coming back?

Never heard from again.

A black kitten crossed my trail.

The name of my beloved is Irrecuperable. Liar.

Albert Ayler at the Village Vanguard. The way to listen is to stop focusing on the notes, he says. Listen to the sound inside the sound.

I brushed on nipple rouge this morning.

In the evening I scrubbed it off.

Devour me.

You said, *Two men are inside me. Remember*

the other one. The one who did not do this to you.

The sound inside the sound.

Eternally en route.

Like a dog is ripping my heart out.

This music I cannot listen to, it makes me dizzy.

The pendulum swinging stably in space while under it, the floor is carried around by the earth's rotation.

Yesterday the snow came, bearing no message.

The wooden chair on which you sat at your desk.

How you wrapped your shins behind the front legs.

Empty of you. Dormant.

Who was it who ravished me? Who ravaged me?

Your thumb stroking the nape of my neck.

The membrane separating me from oblivion has ruptured.

How could you betray yourself like that?

Like that.

When the mower hits the mint.

In a sandwich bag in the freezer, a belted king-fisher.

Flew into the windshield. I thought we could bury it together.

They are wrong who tell me otherwise. It will not be all right.

Villon, shivering and hungry and still going to his desk to write, finding the inkwell frozen solid.

A cockroach on the kitchen wall. It would be blasphemy to keep house.

That mentholated C-flat of your laugh. Its

intervallic swoop into the upper registers,

your eyes closed. Tearing.

You laughed like a rollercoaster.

Completely infectious.

Coltrane's *Meditations*. The dissonance leads to a modulation.

Cat got your tongue?

A downy woodpecker eyes me at the window. Each illumination, another kind of shadow.

As if the light—

A photograph of you that I pore over

looking for clues to what would happen.

What happened?

Can you whisper it to me or have you fallen
asleep?

One last breath leaving the circle of your teeth.

You are strange in my dreams.

I hollow inward. I've gone dark as a hedge.

What a completely outrageous mockingbird.

Purgatory this place, and I, a wraith

wandering lost.

A wraith.

And this photograph I did not take of you

with your arm crossing your chest,

your hand cupping your shoulder

as though it stoppered a wound:

of whom is it a photograph now?

The house finch wiping its beak against the empty tray of the feeder.

Still walking in my socks around the house as though I wouldn't wake you,

not letting all my weight down.

Carrying the unbearably heavy last words I said to you.

As I am going under.

Purgatory this place.

As if the light had stopped in the air.

My sweet.

When you were.

Les:
Outtakes from the Film Interview

I don't know. Until you're emptied out and chucked to the side of the road. To anyone you have something to give. I try not to judge someone's need, you usually can't anyway.

*

To be consequent to my friends.

*

So the Nixons and Unferths of the world roll out of bed, they look in the mirror and see their mug in the tain. And they think they're some kind of radiance surrounded by fog. The genius among pissants. And they think about their desert loneliness, how isolated and heroic they are, surrounded by a lesser race of men. You've seen that kind of man, we all have. But I'm going down with the ones in the mead house snoring and dreaming on the benches.

*

An ordinary man. With an exigency, I guess.

*

To buy a ruined mill town, say like Old Dawt

in Ozark County, and invite all my friends to move in. Jobs first come first serve. Who wants to be postmaster? Who'll run the café? The excellent company I've been privileged to know—I'd love to seem them fall together in some such place.

*

For my conviction and my action to be of a piece.

*

Yeah, but the ones who think they've got the right to speak, the gift of tongues, the kiss-my-holier-than-thou title deed and some indisputable angle on everything that's happening—those righteous motherfuckers when you get to know them, they're hollow as an egret bone.

*

Oh, when you get down to the licklog, just to be a good friend. To be consequent to those around me. I guess I can't see any virtue higher than that.

*

Almost all my so-called discoveries, like it or not, have come about through some kind of violence.

*

Sure, art doesn't save anybody the way a sack of rice does. But that doesn't mean it's worthless. There're plenty of ways of living in the world and among words and some of them are a fuck of a lot more predatory than others.

*

You'd like to think paying more attention to language might help keep you from being cornholed by frauds. To die for your country, a lot of Americans heard that and they stood up and saluted. But what it means and how it means and who is saying it and who is dying it—I'd like to think there is some hope anyway to be found in paying attention to the words.

*

To be unreflective about language, you limit the frequencies of meaning and even, I'd say, of experience. The newspaper, that's one frequency, obsessed with selling something, an Olivieri fur coat or a story about embezzlement. Sequences of so-called facts running across our eyeballs like lemmings.

*

Remember Jimmy Cliff saying, *Hero no can die
'til last scene, man.* But no one scripts their own last
scene. And no one's congruent with anything more
than what they came with. I know, now and then
some people break through. Take on the weight of
whatever it might mean that we come to call them
heroes. But maybe that happens less from looking
into the horizon than from being present for what's
at hand.

*

Who'd say they didn't have regrets? It's like
what if tomorrow you're walking up the street and
some bad-ass dog comes tearing around the hedge
as though it's waited its whole life for you. Your
leg's in its mouth, you're kicking and screaming
Jesus Christ freaking out on the sidewalk in panic
and pure pain, maybe you can just make out some
woman behind the hedge calling the dog in a
singsong voice like she thinks it's still sleeping
under the porch and it's time for the dog's breakfast. And some kernel in the back of your mind is
wondering how you came into this situation, it's so
random, you just happened to make your way down
to the corner to pick up milk right then, the gate
was left open, you were walking on this side of the
street to get a load of the paulownia in bloom in the
banker's yard. But it's just the same as your determined interview with me. It may seem like you're

asking me questions you've long intended to ask and of course that's true in part. But the sequence of random inconsequential incidents that led you here—the time two years ago when you braked to keep from running over a turtle that turned out to be the punt of a beer bottle in the road, that instant when reaching for a book, another book near it on the shelf caught your attention, the Friday night you took a right on the way home when you might have gone straight—those forgotten, stupid, inconsequential moments form beds of substrate underlying all the logic on the surface.

*

Think of all the shit that insulates us from the real encounter. When Rimbaud writes *I is another*, I for one always figured he meant I is the imaginary. Your sense of self, my sense of self, it's always imagined. Constructed. We can't picture some objective reality any more than a photograph pictures what's there, right? You know people in tribes that haven't seen photographs, when they see one, even one that shows them their own face, they don't always recognize the image. It's miniature and flat and maybe black and white and it doesn't have a smell, and the kick of being isn't in it at all.

*

We want to seize the world and make our own way in it and we're full of intention but we're completely unprepared. Because each moment we come into contact with others, and not just with others but with things and events and ourselves, our knee going out, or a childhood memory popping up freshly hatched when we had no idea we'd been carrying it, incubating it all this time, it was part of us, just as DNA from former parasites very early in our history as a species—did you know this?—became integrated in our own DNA, we're mongrels at the core, which is why anyone's notion of racial purity is bullshit. We can't even make claims for the purity of our species, much less our so-called race. We're involved in each other in ways and at levels that no one figured, and each moment is unpredictable, hotwired with interconnections that make us forever vulnerable. We don't know what will happen, we aren't alone at the wheel, despite our best efforts, we're at risk, but that vulnerability is all we'll ever know of the sacred, it's what we don't comprehend and what calls us to be responsible for others, for everything, the source spring of what we call our conscience. And all that feeling of interrelation and vulnerability is enough to scare anyone, so we fight it off, we cultivate boredom, we try to assert control by talking shit, talking shop, doing the same old same old, sopping up the impersonal drone of facts, newspapers, sales pitches, the disembodied language of real indifference that eclipses poetry every time. Poetry with its subterranean insights and amphetamine rushes lighting us up, lighting up whatever it is we call our inner selves, that holy knot that gives us a hold on what we actually feel. So, yeah, we imitate others, we say nothing much is happening, nothing's going on, just the usual, *comme ci comme ça*, how bout you, the rain looks like rain and the river sounds like a river. But, you know, if you hold still and listen to the river up around Calico Rock, you can *hear* silt scouring the boulders. Scouring them like a motherfucker. And that part of the river doesn't sound like any other river. None of it sounds like anywhere else. Last week, we were up there, I saw a fisherman reel in a little sun perch and drag it up onto the sand and bend down with his bait knife to slice the tail off, and then, while it flopped by his boots, he skewered the tail with his hook and threw the line back into the river to catch a bigger fish. My guess would be that ethics comes from imagination, from the imagination of something or someone else suffering. There's no given.

*

Giotto, he can paint the mountains in the background of the "Betrayal of Christ" because rocks from those very mountains have been crushed and stirred up into the pigments he's using. You know, in a synagogue, a reader of the Torah doesn't touch the scroll with his hand. As soon as we make contact with the sacred, we're face to face with death and we have to ask ourselves who we are. And everything is like that. That's the way we're born into the next minute. Of course, I know every step I've taken has had repercussions. I know I've hurt people I love. I'm sorry for it and I don't see the point in defending myself. Other things I've done I'll never know about, even if what I did burrows into some stranger like a chigger and brings them misery for years. Or joy. Even if I try to weigh it all out ahead of time, even if I stay in the bathroom sitting on the toilet, I can't avoid setting off consequences I would never, ever countenance. I can't even be sure of the immediate effects of what I *think* I set into motion. We can't be sure. Of ourselves or others. Which is the stunning beauty of it, like they say. Maybe the best we can do is try to leave ourselves unprotected. To keep brushing off habits, how we see things and what we expect, as they crust around us. Brushing the green flies of *the usual* off the tablecloth. To pay attention. To get a whiff of the stinking rich shit of the real. To approach each other and the world with as much vulnerability as we can possibly sustain. To open out. With all our mind and body and imagination, to keep opening out.

*

Like I said. As a poet. As a friend.

ACKNOWLEDGMENTS

"Everyone knows how much I love you.
All your gestures
Have become my gestures."
Variation on a translation by Kenneth Rexroth of an
anonymous Japansese poem.

"Landscape with a Man Being Killed by a Snake,"
the title of a painting by Nicholas Poussin.

"How can I find you in that stupendous blaze"
is derived from a line by Aaron Shabtai,
translated by Peter Cole.

At ease in honesty, derived from Albert Camus's
notebooks.

I never know when you think I'm interesting,
derived from André Gide's notebooks.

"Gone Klimpt" wrote the poet Ronald Johnson.

I listen to what I can leave out: Miles Davis said it.

"There are bright moments"—the riff comes from
"Bright Moments Song" on Rahsaan Roland Kirk's
album, *Bright Moments*, Atlantic Records, 1973.